# POP MONSTERS
## The Modern-Day Craze for Vampires and Werewolves

# THE MAKING OF A MONSTER
# Vampires & Werewolves

# POP MONSTERS
## The Modern-Day Craze for Vampires and Werewolves

by Emily Sanna

Mason Crest Publishers

MASON CREST PUBLISHERS INC.
370 Reed Road
Broomall, Pennsylvania 19008
(866)MCP-BOOK (toll free)
www.masoncrest.com

First Printing
9 8 7 6 5 4 3 2 1

ISBN (series) 978-1-4222-1801-3
Paperback ISBN (series) 978-1-4222-1954-6

Library of Congress Cataloging-in-Publication Data
Sanna, Emily
 Pop monsters : the modern-day craze for vampires and werewolves / by Emily Sanna.
      p. cm.
 Includes bibliographical references and index.
 ISBN 978-1-4222-1806-8 (hardcover)    ISBN 978-1-4222-1959-1 (pbk.)
 1. Vampires. 2.  Werewolves.  I. Title.
 BF1556.S25 2011
 398'.45—dc22
                                                    2010025186

Produced by Harding House Publishing Service, Inc.
www.hardinghousepages.com
Interior design by MK Bassett-Harvey.
Cover design by Torque Advertising + Design.
Printed in the USA by Bang Printing.

# CONTENTS

# chapter 1
# OUR FASCINATION WITH VAMPIRES AND WEREWOLVES

**B**ooks, movies, or television shows like *Twilight* or *Buffy the Vampire Slayer* are nothing new. Monsters, including vampires and werewolves, have fascinated people for hundreds, if not thousands, of years. Some of the earliest myths include stories of people who can turn into animals or who have special connections to the supernatural realm. For example, one legend says that the founders of ancient Rome, the twins Romulus and Remus, were raised by a wolf and a woodpecker, who cared for the infants until a human woodcutter found them and could adopt them. While these kinds of stories have been around almost as long as humans have, stories like this gained a new popularity with the rise of cheap, mass-produced literature and the film industry.

# Werewolves and Us

If anything, the concept of werewolves has been around longer than that of vampires. Since the beginning of agricultural society, humans have had a complicated relationship with wolves. Wolves could inspire both fear and awe; wolves sometimes stole children and livestock, but they were also the first animal to become domesticated, and they were respected for their power and independence.

Unlike vampires, who historically have been portrayed as purely evil characters, werewolves are often portrayed more sympathetically. They struggle to contain their dualities, the animal and human sides of their natures. In many ways, the full moon, the symbol of the werewolf's impending transition from human to wolf, serves as an apt metaphor for the werewolf's life. Moonlight, the opposite of daylight, is associated with the dark, the strange, the unfamiliar, and all that is unknown and mysterious.

## The Modern Psychology of Werewolves' Allure

Some people argue that the idea of the werewolf reflects women's attraction to males who cannot be tamed.

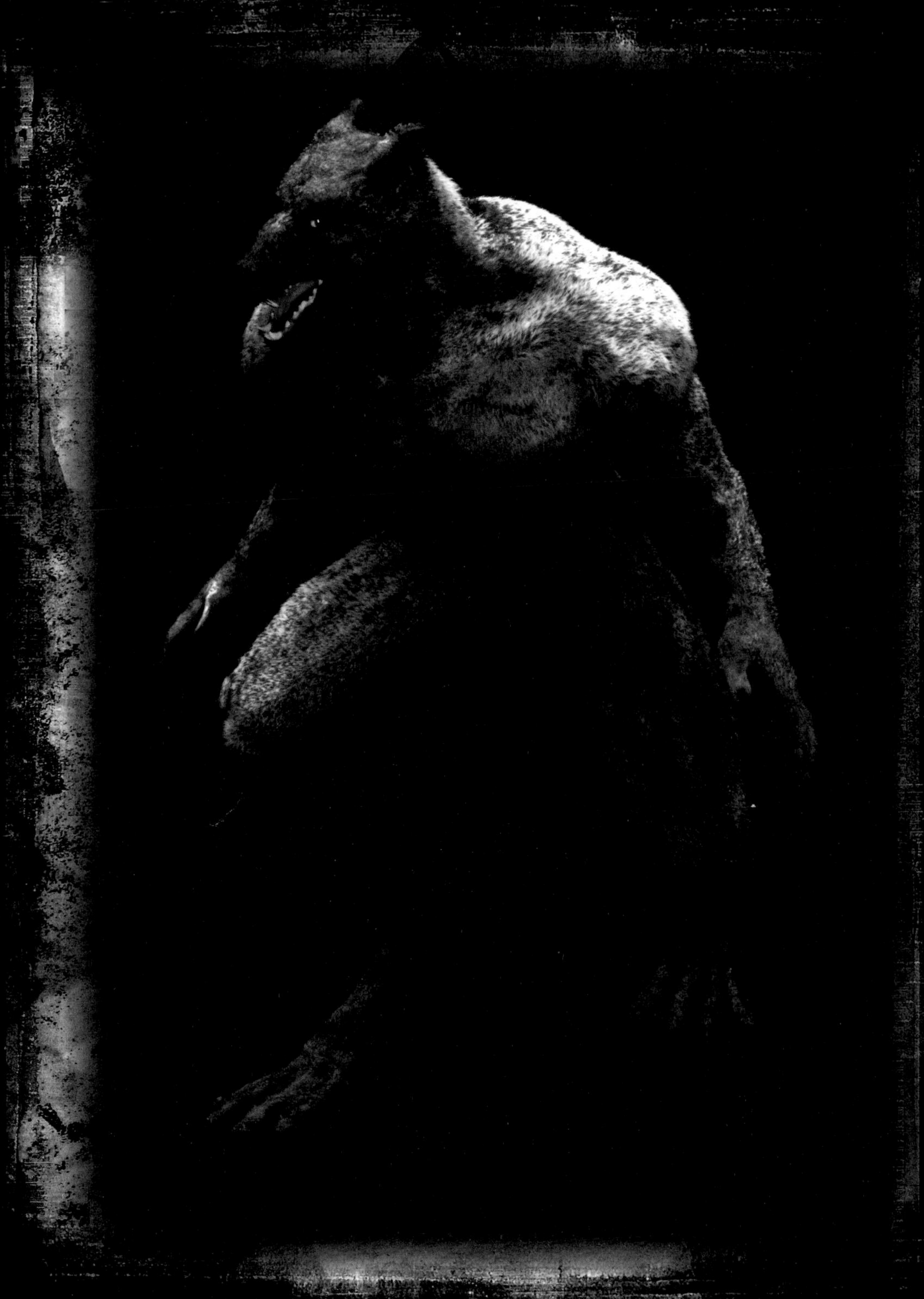

After all, people who cannot control their own physical aggression have always been men! And yet, at the same time, our modern attraction to werewolves has to do with their inner conflict. Werewolves are not purely evil, at least not most of the time. They are able to fall in love, to feel for the people they have harmed, and to feel remorse, even if it is after the fact. A werewolf is the ultimate "bad boy," the dangerous male women love to hate.

Another hypothesis for the recent rise in werewolves' popularity turns to the current controversies over genetic modification. Genetically modified crops are now easily available, giving rise to questions not only of environmental consequences but also of morality. Do we as humans have the right to influence the natural course of evolution? If we do genetic testing to show the possibility of an unborn child having certain diseases, will that lead to someday testing to see what color hair or eyes a baby will have—and getting rid of fetuses that don't measure up to their parents' list of preferences? Is this an acceptable use of technology? What about the "mutant" plants that are being created—crops that contain the DNA of other kinds of plants, or even animals, which make them more able to withstand high temperatures or little water? While these have all been created in an attempt to bring food to areas where it is hard to grow, what are the limits on this type of technology? The werewolf, which is by definition a half-human, half-animal hybrid, brings these fears to the forefront of our minds. What does it mean to be human? Can we learn the answer to this question from werewolf stories?

# Werewolves in Films and Movies

While there are depictions of werewolves as purely malevolent creatures, many times they are normal, likable human beings who happen to have a problem they must deal with once a month, when the moon turns full. For example, in the Harry Potter series, by J.K Rowling, Professor Remus Lupin is a werewolf (as the reader finds out at the end of the third book). The famous (and entirely evil) Fenrir Greyback bit Lupin when he was a child, and so Lupin must transform into a wolf at every full moon. However, thanks to a potion made by Professor Snape, most of the time Lupin is able to keep control over his base emotions, even in his wolf form, and thus keep from killing any innocent people. Throughout the series, he struggles with his identity, for a while refusing to be in a relationship with Nymphadora Tonks—although he later marries her and has a son—because of his affliction. However, the fact that he is a werewolf seems to bother him more than it does any of the other characters, who accept him as a good professor, friend, and overall caring human being.

Another werewolf in popular culture is Oz, a character in *Buffy the Vampire Slayer*. In the show, Oz's younger cousin bites him while he is in high school, transforming him into a werewolf. Precautions must be taken during the three nights around the full moon (for a while Oz is locked up in the library with one of the other main characters standing guard but most of the time he is able to live a full life; he is a member of a band called Dingoes Ate My Baby, and he has a relationship with Willow, a witch who is one of the other main characters.

This sympathetic portrayal of werewolves goes back to the show *The Munsters*, where Eddie Munster, the only child of Herman and Lily, was a werewolf. Despite this, he was also in fifth grade at a public school, won ribbons for track competitions, had a favorite doll (a werewolf named Woof Woof), and boasted of his ability to open tin cans with his ears.

# Vampires and the Rise of Gothic Literature

The Gothic novel was a form of literature that was popular in England in the late eighteenth and early nineteenth centuries. In many cases, it was a reaction against the standard form of writing during that time, which was highly structured. While other popular novels focused on the themes of love, freedom, and social liberation, the Gothic movement attempted to portray the decline of the world, focusing more on fear and

The Gothic literature of the nineteenth century was full of brooding castles, death, ghosts, and dark, mysterious women.

destruction. In many cases, this led to a different kind of formula in plot, setting, and characterization. For example, the setting was often in old ruined buildings, places that had once been expensive and beautiful but were now falling apart. The hero or heroines were isolated from their friends and family, and placed at the mercies of the villain, who was the epitome of evil. The plot devices prevalent in this genre made it easy to introduce characters like vampires or werewolves, both of which fell easily into the villain roles.

The Gothic novel was meant to bridge the gap between the imaginary and the realistic, something that was easy to illustrate using human monsters. Vampires are both people, with human emotions and feelings, and supernatural. One side of their personality can be stressed over the other, but they are always shown as contradictory. (In a similar way, werewolves must always struggle between their human and wolf natures.) It was because these characters could epitomize these human contradictions that they were so popular. Readers could acknowledge issues with which they themselves were dealing without these issues hitting as close to home. They could feel both excited and disgusted at the same time, without feeling guilty for enjoying the story.

Since the Victorian era, when the Gothic novel became popular, the motives of vampires have changed as society has developed and has had new issues to confront.

For example, vampires today are rarely portrayed as aristocrats, as they were in Bram Stoker's *Dracula* or other early vampire stories. However, we can still identify with their struggles to adapt to a world that doesn't accept them for who they are.

A recent television show, *True Blood*, played on the attraction we feel toward vampires. In the show, which is based on the Southern Vampire Mystery series by Charlaine Harris, a parallel is made between the vampire characters and issues that real-life LGBT (lesbian, gay, bisexual, and transgender) groups are dealing with today. In *True Blood*, the vampires have all recently come "out of the coffin," a term that is intentionally connected to "coming out of the closet." They are struggling for civil rights, to prove to the rest of society that they are no less worthy of being contributing members of society as the rest of the human population.

Although the way of connecting to human struggles and fears has changed since Victorian times, vampires still manage to make us examine our own insecurities, all the while letting us hold these issues at a distance because of the supernatural aspect of vampires' lives.

# Early Vampire Literature

The first vampire story was written by John Polidori and titled, quite aptly, "The Vampyre." The story deals with two men, Lord Ruthven and Aubrey; Ruthven destroys all the people around him while Aubrey watches. Women

# THE STORY BEHIND THE STORY

"The Vampyre" was written at the same time as another Gothic classic, Mary Shelley's *Frankenstein*. A few writer friends, including Polidori, Mary Shelley and her husband Percy, and Lord Byron, had gone to the mountains for a vacation. While there, they amused themselves by telling each other horror stories. While Mary Shelley told what would later become *Frankenstein*, Lord Byron told a story about a vampire. Byron had no desire to take his story any further, so Polidori picked it up and turned it into a novel, later publishing it under Byron's name in 1819. When Byron found out, he called the publisher and demanded that his name be taken off the book. While the story can be read merely as a story about a purely evil vampire and the helpless humans around him, many people have suggested that Ruthven and Aubrey are based on Byron and Polidori, respectively.

fall in love with him, and he refuses to marry them (a big deal in Victorian England, where a woman's reputation was ruined if she was found to have had any relationship with a man who wasn't related to her), while men become addicted to gambling and other immoral pursuits. Halfway through the story, Aubrey realizes that Ruthven is a vampire, and that the way he spreads evil illustrates his lack of humanity, his total unconcern for anyone other than himself.

## Penny Dreadfuls: A Different Kind of Vampire Story

Not all Gothic vampire stories were written for the educated elite. Some were intended instead for younger and less privileged audiences. "Penny dreadfuls," as they were called, were illustrated stories created for mass production. They were sold to young readers on cheap paper (therefore the cost of a penny) and were illustrated with woodcut illustrations, much like the later comic books.

One series, titled "Varney the Vampire," told the story of a vampire named Sir Francis Varney, and his misadventures, mostly dealing with his attempts to attack the Bannerworth family. While he starts off as a purely evil character, over the span of the series (which lasted for two years in the 1840s), he becomes more sympathetic. The reader eventually learns that he was somehow turned into a vampire as a punishment for his sins.

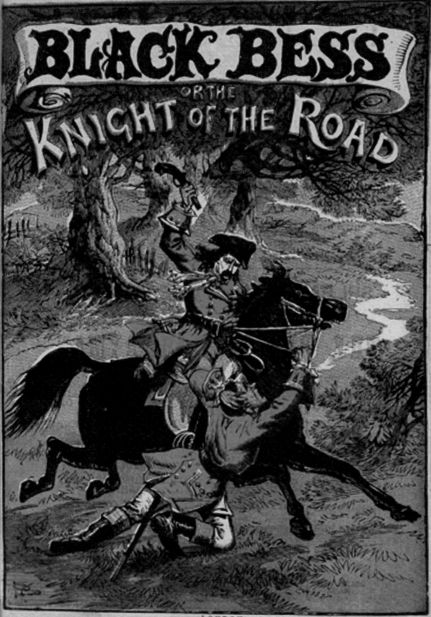

Nos. 1 & 2, and a MAGNIFICENT PICTURE, PRINTED IN COLOURS,
TURPIN LEAPS BESS OVER THE HORSES OF THE MAIL COACH.

# BLACK BESS

## OR THE

# KNIGHT OF THE ROAD

LONDON:
Published by E. HARRISON, and Sold by all Newsagents everywhere.
PRICE ONE PENNY.

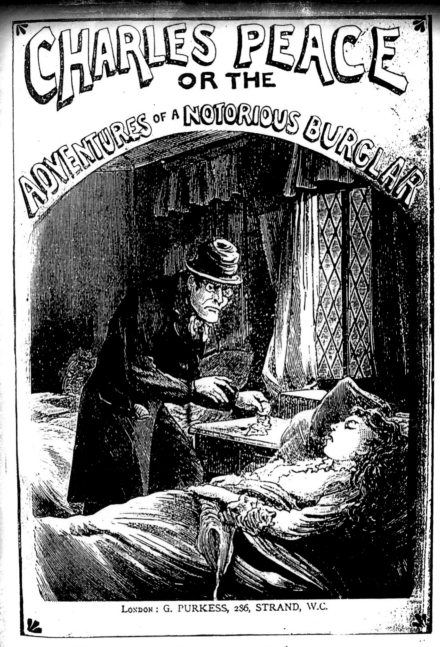

Penny dreadfuls were a cross between comic books and the National Enquirer type of magazine you see while you're standing in line at the grocery store. They were sensationalist and cheaply produced, intended for ordinary people.

He committed various political treasons and killed his own son. In the end of the series, he is unable to make restitution or deal with his own remorse, and he eventually throws himself into a volcano, thereby ending his life as an immortal vampire destined to kill people for their blood. This story, while not as literary-minded as "The Vampyre," had a much larger audience and was able to bring vampires into the public consciousness.

# Dracula

No book dealing with vampires would be complete without at least mentioning Bram Stoker's novel *Dracula*. This book has become immortalized in both literature and film, and Western culture took from it many of its clichés about what vampires are and what they can do. For example, *Dracula* gave us our ideas about vampires hating garlic and crosses, being able to be killed by a stake through the heart, not being able to enter a house without being invited, having no shadows or reflections, and having to sleep near their native earth.

Like many other Gothic novelists, Stoker was able to address many of the current issues of his time. His characters deal with issues like the struggle between modernity and superstition, and the question of women's rights and sexuality.

One of the characters, Van Helsing, is a professor who is one of the only people who has the knowledge to stop Dracula. He uses modern science and medicine, as well as folklore and superstition, in his attempt. Different sources argue over which side (modernity or superstition) comes out successful in the end, or whether they both contribute to the final demise of Dracula, but it can be argued that Van Helsing is an example of the conflict between modern technology and the old ways of life.

Women's roles in society are also examined by highlighting the differences between the two female characters. One woman, Mina Murray, who later goes on to marry Jonathan Harker and have a child, is portrayed as the ultimate Victorian woman. She is feminine and chaste, remaining the perfect virtuous woman throughout the book. Lucy Westenra, on the other hand, is portrayed as too sexual and voluptuous. While she attempts to remain pure, her beauty results in her conversion into a vampire. Her new vampire-hood results in freedom for her in many ways (much like the women during that time who were fighting for suffrage and other rights, it could be argued), Stoker portrays this freedom as unrestrained sexual behavior, a behavior that is only cured with Lucy's death.

Through Stoker's characterizations of women and others, he is able to deal with current issues in his novel, just like many of the other Gothic novelists. However, despite this social commentary, it was not until the movies were made that *Dracula* became an internationally known phenomenon.

# CHRISTOPHER LEE

Christopher Lee was born in 1922 in London. He attended Eton, and later Wellington College, after which he worked as an office clerk until World War II, when he enlisted in the Royal Air Force (RAF). After the war, Lee started working as an actor, getting small parts in films like **Hamlet**, **Corridor of Mirrors**, and **Moulin Rouge**. In the late 1950s, with his role as Dracula in a number of films, Lee finally achieved stardom.

Lee, perhaps even more than Bela Lugosi, is known for his roles as a villain. While he has starred in some mainstream films, like the Bond film **The Man with the Golden Gun** (1974), he remains most famous for his roles as Dracula, Saruman (in the **Lord of the Rings** trilogy), Count Dooku (in **Star Wars Episode II: Attack of the Clones**), and, most recently, as the voice of the Jabberwocky in **Alice in Wonderland**.

*Christopher Lee as the British Dracula.*

# The *Dracula* Films

The first Dracula movie came out in 1931, directed by Tod Browning and starring Bela Lugosi as Dracula. While it was criticized as being too stiff and lacking in special effects and cinematography, it was still a huge success. Much of this may have depended on the actors, who were all fairly successful outside this film. (Poor Lugosi could never find a role that was not based on his acting as Dracula, however; for the rest of his life he was type-cast as villains.) For whatever reason, the film was successful, and it prompted Universal Studios to put out a whole series of monster movies based on that first *Dracula*. These included such films as *Dracula's Daughter* (1936), *Son of Dracula* (1943), and *House of Dracula* (1945). These movies had little or nothing to do with Stoker's actual book besides the main characters, but the idea of Dracula and the role of vampires soon expanded beyond the novel to take on a life of their own.

While Universal had the rights to the Dracula franchise in the United States, in Britain a series of films were produced titled the *British Hammer Horror Series*. The first of these was *Dracula*, starring Christopher Lee in his iconic role. Lee's Dracula was a success because he was able to portray the contradictions that are so popular in vampires' personalities; he was aristocratic with a sense of humor, and yet deeply and totally evil.

Both Lee and Lugosi's portrayals of vampires produced the concept of vampires as aristocratic and attractive, yet inhuman and evil. This portrayal of vampires as purely evil lasted into nearly the twenty-first century, with stories like *Buffy*, whose main character's purpose in life is to protect society from the vampires who want to destroy it. Not until late in the twentieth century did new ideas about vampires develop. These vampires were sympathetic characters with a certain kind of sexual appeal.

# chapter 2
# THE RISE OF THE SEXY MONSTER

The person who has had the most impact on how vampires are portrayed in today's culture has been Anne Rice. Born Howard Allen O'Brien, Rice has written vampire stories over the course of more than twenty-five years. While today she has stopped writing about the vampires Lestat and Louis, and has focused solely on religious novels, including several biographies of Jesus Christ, her previous work remains important, both to Rice's identity as an author and to pop culture in general. Her imagination helped us all transform our vision of vampires from Count Dracula, the menacing aristocrat, to Edward Cullen, the teenage vampire in Stephanie Meyer's Twilight series who has made thousands, if not millions, of young girls fall in love with him.

# Anne Rice's Vampires

Most of Anne Rice's vampire stories are grouped in a series called The Vampire Chronicles. The first of these books, *Interview with a Vampire*, was published in 1976, while the last, titled *Blood Canticle*, came out in 2002. While the books are about different characters, they all take place in the same world and focus around the life of one vampire in particular, Lestat.

In the Chronicles, some of the qualities of the characters might seem familiar to readers who have read older books like *Dracula*, but other characteristics are completely different. Gone are the vampires who are vanquished by garlic, crosses, and stakes through the heart. Instead, the only way a vampire can be killed is through direct exposure to sunlight (and this only works if a vampire is young—that is, under 1,000 years old). While these new vampires do need blood, they can also drink animal blood if human blood is unavailable or if they choose to abstain from human blood for moral reasons. Instead of having magical powers, Rice's vampires merely have extreme physical prowess; they can move extremely quickly and have greater senses of smell, sight, and hearing. Rice's physical descriptions of her characters have also influenced how vampires

*Author Anne Rice made the sexy vampire a part of mainstream culture.*

have been portrayed in the literature since then; she describes their skin as pale and their eyes as glowing.

In Rice's books, as with later vampiric characters, vampirism is portrayed as both a gift and a curse. While vampires are blessed with keener senses and enormously powerful bodies, they also must drink blood in order to survive. Rice's vampires must struggle between their human and undead natures. They are humans in that they are emotionally dependent on the relationships they have with others, and yet in order to have these relationships, they must repress their incredible hunger and desire to kill.

# True Blood

The HBO series *True Blood* plays on the image, spread by Anne Rice, of the sexy vampire, a being who can have human relationships (although this is done only with difficulty in many cases). The television show is based on a series of novels by Charlaine Harris titled The Southern Vampire Mysteries. The TV episodes follow the life of Sookie Stackhouse, a waitress at a bar who just happens to be able to hear people's thoughts. One day, she meets Bill Compton; intrigued because she can't hear what's going on inside his head, she eventually learns that he is a 173-year-old vampire. As could be predicted, they end up falling in love, which leads to interesting conflicts as Sookie tries to explain her new boyfriend to her family and friends, while Bill must fight the vampire community in order to get them to see Sookie as a person rather than as food or an instrument to be utilized for their own gain.

In the *True Blood* world, a Japanese company has just released a drink called TruBlood, synthetic blood that allows vampires to exist without killing humans for their blood. This leads to vampires "coming out of the coffin," while humans now are forced to realize that vampires

# BARNABAS COLLINS OF *DARK SHADOWS*

Even before Anne Rice, the Gothic soap opera **Dark Shadows** brought to life during the 1960s and 1970s a sexy, brooding vampire named Barnabas Collins, played by Jonathan Frid. In addition to vampires, *Dark Shadows* featured werewolves, ghosts, zombies, man-made monsters, witches, warlocks, time travel (both into the past and into the future), and a parallel universe. As a teenager, actor Johnny Depp was so fascinated by the show that he wanted to *be* Barnabas Collins—and he has gotten his chance in the twenty-first-century movie version of the cult classic, produced by Tim Burton.

Thou shall not crave thy neighbor.

# TRUEBLOOD ℠

A NEW SERIES FROM THE CREATOR OF **SIX FEET UNDER**

# INTERVIEW WITH A VAMPIRE: THE MOVIE

In 1994, Neil Jordan directed a movie version of the first book in the Vampire Chronicles. The film starred Brad Pitt as Louis and Tom Cruise as the vampire Lestat. Kirsten Dunst was also in the film as the child vampire Claudia. While the movie was nominated for two Oscars (for best set direction and for best original score), some critics complained that the movie was too gruesome and bloody. Oprah Winfrey was one of these; she stormed out of the premier because of the amount of blood.

really do exist. Of course, this leads to all kind of interesting conflicts, as the relationships between humans and the supernatural vampires are explored and defined. And the rise of the vampires means that other supernatural creatures can show themselves as well; in the first two seasons of *True Blood*, the audience learns that one of the characters is a shape shifter, while a maenad attempts to hypnotize the whole community in order to achieve her goals and bring back the god Dionysius to Earth.

The vampires in *True Blood* are much like those described by Anne Rice, both in physical characteristics and powers. They are extremely pale and supernaturally beautiful. They can run faster than the human eye can see, and they also can manipulate humans through hypnosis or by putting them into a sort of trance. They do not show any revulsion toward garlic (although the humans in the show seem to think they should). However, silver does have the capacity to severely weaken them; they won't die unless they are shot with a silver bullet, but silver will make them unable to act or respond to situations. (In many cases, silver affects vampires like kryptonite does Superman.) The vampires in *True Blood* seem easier to kill than the ones in The Vampire Chronicles. While they still couldn't exactly be described as easy to get rid of, a silver bullet, wooden stake, or fire will result in their death, as well as direct sunlight. According to Rice, only young vampires can really be killed by sunlight, although it will weaken all of them; in *True Blood*, however, the age of the vampire doesn't matter: the oldest vampire in the show, Godric, who is 2,000 years old, eventually kills himself by standing in the light of the rising sun.

While the abilities of the vampires in *True Blood* may differ slightly from those in Anne Rice's novels, the overall picture of them has not changed. They remain beings

that are set apart from humans and are yet appealing. The reasons for this have been suggested in the previous chapter, but no one can quite pin down exactly why vampires and other monsters are so popular. Something about the inherent contradictions within their beings intrigues and excites us. Anne Rice used this attraction to build an image of vampires as beings with incredible sex appeal.

# Sexy Werewolves

Perhaps the most famous sexy werewolf in popular culture today is Jacob from the Twilight series, which will be discussed in more depth in a later chapter. Teenagers (and some adults too!) have fought about who is more attractive in the book, the vampire or the werewolf, declaring themselves to be on either "Team Jacob" or "Team Edward." But even before *Twilight* and the rise of the teenage supernatural being, werewolves were seen as appealing. There is a sort of inherent, appealing mystery in werewolves. Are they human or animal? How do they relate to the animal world? (And how does this illustrate how humanity in general relates to the natural world?)

The werewolf allows people, mainly men, to escape the bonds of humanity and to act in ways that would normally be taboo. The monster we all have within is allowed to come out. We embrace its presence, rather

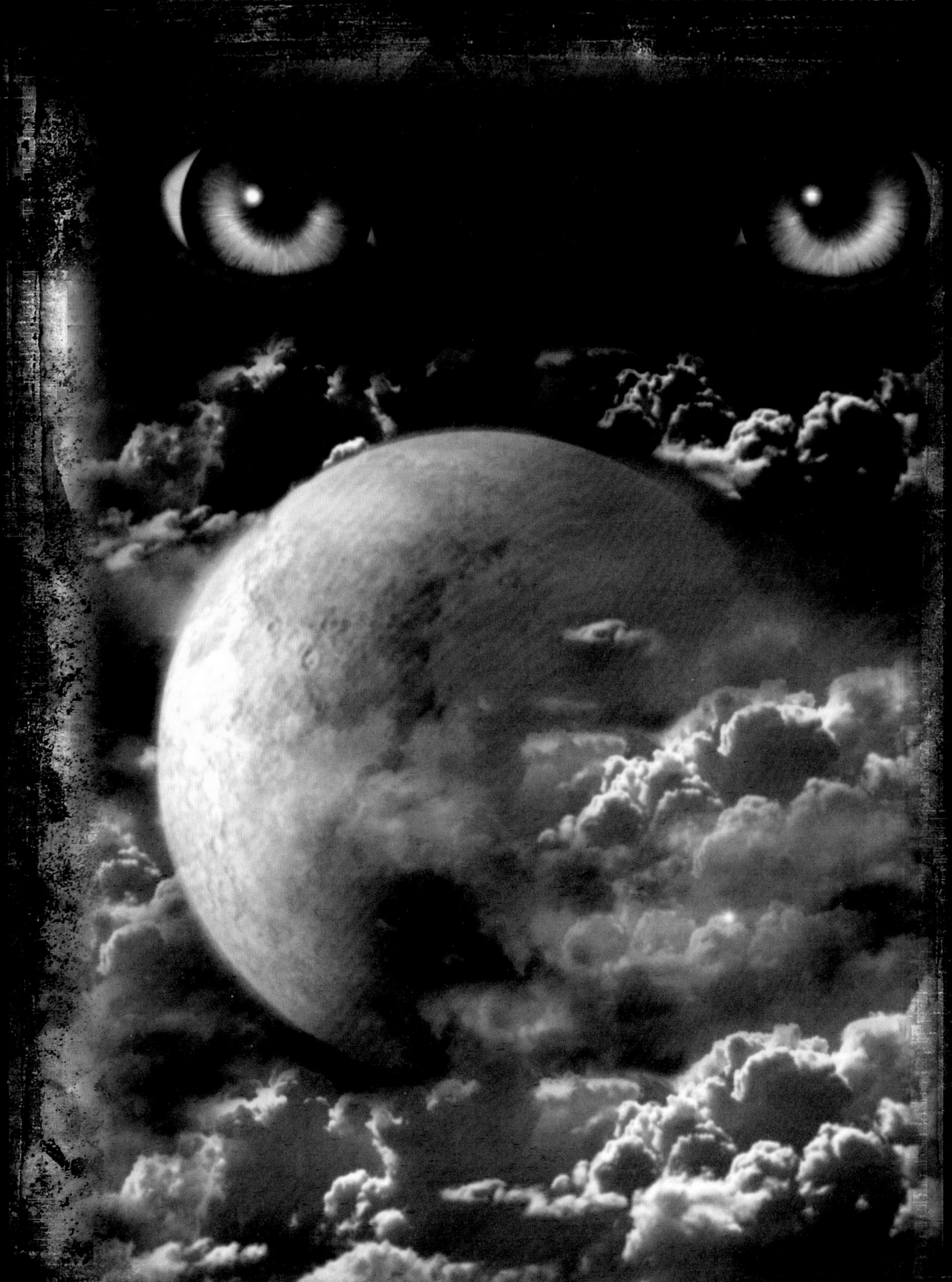

than ignore that it exists at all. To say something is monstrous is oftentimes a different way of saying something is different or doesn't fit in; to be monstrous or forbidden is not necessarily to be evil. Oftentimes, these werewolf heroes find ways to integrate their wolf natures with their human natures, thereby becoming complete human beings. To add an environmental twist to the issue, as werewolves becoming more in touch with their animal side, they also become closer to the Earth and the environment than most people are.

# Where Are the Women Werewolves?

Characters in the Harry Potter books, *Buffy the Vampire Slayer*, *True Blood*, and the Twilight series are all male werewolves. But can you think of a female werewolf? Sure, there is the one female werewolf character in the Twilight series, but she is only mentioned as an aside and never as a main part of the story.

One academic scholar, Elizabeth Clark, talks about this lack of female werewolves in popular culture. She argues that although werewolves allow us to examine human behavior and roles in society, we still do so through a very conservative lens; traditional ways of behaving are still maintained. Men still act like men, and women still act like women—men are the animalistic creatures controlled by their own baser natures, while women are the ones with whom the wolves fall in love, thereby achieving salvation through their feelings for a woman. Society looks at these plot devices and finds them appealing. If, on the other hand, it were the woman who was the wolf, too many of our ideas about how society should work would be broken. Showing a large, extremely hairy woman who is physically aggressive is not sexually appealing to most people; instead, many people think it's just gross! We are taught that while men can be large and hairy and physically overwhelming, this is not an appropriate model for women to take—or, if they do take on these roles, they cannot be physically or sexually attractive.

In the few cases where there are female werewolves (Clark cites some examples on *Buffy* and the spin-off show *Angel*), physical and emotional aggressiveness must be balanced. In many cases, Clark argues, this is done by showing that the women may be physically or sexually aggressive, but they are still extremely physically beautiful—at least when still in human form. The female body, as the epitome of physical beauty, is rarely connected to the hairy, monster's body.

While the image of both vampires and werewolves as sexually appealing is a dominant model in today's society, it is not the only depiction of these creatures. In one iconic show, *Buffy the Vampire Slayer*, the vampires are not attractive at all. Instead, they are grotesque creatures with almost no personality outside of their desire to kill all humans.

## chapter 3
# THE BUFFY CULT

While no book that talks about popular culture and vampires would be complete without mentioning *Buffy the Vampire Slayer*, in many ways this television series doesn't fit in with what we have to say in the rest of the book. The show focuses more on the human characters—or at least, the characters whose human nature can prevail over their supernatural ones. The vampires are all portrayed as soulless villains, totally evil beings who have no goal in mind except the extermination of the human race. Unlike the vampires in Anne Rice's books or *True Blood*, these vampires have no desire to have human relationships or to relate to humans at all. Instead, they are demons, inhabiting human bodies to accomplish their own aims. The sole exception in the show is Angel, a vampire who feels regret for his actions and is therefore able to interact with the human characters, even to the extent of having a relationship with Buffy herself. There are other supernatural characters as well, such as Oz, who is a werewolf, but the human side of these characters is continually stressed over their supernatural side.

# Buffy

The show centers on the character of Buffy, who has been destined to be the Slayer, a young girl whose purpose is to save the rest of humanity from the vampires. In the beginning of the series, she moves from Los Angeles to Sunnydale, only to find that her new town is the site of the Hellmouth—a sort of portal into the underworld of demons, vampires, and everything else evil—which provides her and her friends many opportunities to fight the forces of darkness. Throughout the show's seven seasons, the audience follows Buffy through high school and college as she struggles to accept who and what she is, while at the same time she is growing up, having a "normal" teenage life by day while she fights vampires during the night.

Many have suggested, including the writer and director Joss Whedon, that part of the reason why *Buffy* is so popular is that it turns most horror movie plots upside down. Instead of the little girl being the victim (as in stories that range from Little Red Riding Hood to *Dracula*), here the teenage girl has the power and ability to save the rest of humanity from evil. Instead of the heroine

EE THE WORLD

IT'S HOW YOU SEE THE WORLD

being dependent on a man to save her, Buffy instead saves others, including several of the male characters. This role reversal gives girls a positive model to follow, instead of being taught they are always at the mercy of the male characters—whether that be the vampires (who may or may not be physically attracted to them) or the human characters.

# Vampires in *Buffy*

In many ways, the vampires in *Buffy* are more similar to the vampires in old legends than they are to other modern vampires. *Buffy*'s vampires are deathly afraid of crucifixes, and they can also be killed by wooden stakes to the heart or sunlight. In many modern stories, including *True Blood* and Anne Rice's novels, the act of drinking someone's blood creates a sort of mental or spiritual bond between the vampire and his prey. This is not the case in *Buffy*, where blood acts merely as physical sustenance for the vampires. And yet there are a few vampires in the series who, for whatever reason, have more human aspects to their personalities. These vampires are the ones who engage in relationships with the characters.

## Angel

Angel is a vampire with a soul—thereby allowing him to feel remorse for his sins, which motivates him to help

# THE BUFFY CULT

All of the works of literature discussed in this book have been wildly popular. However, **Buffy**, perhaps more than any of the others, has gained something of a cult status. There have been numerous academic articles written about **Buffy**—not just about the effects of the show on contemporary culture, but on the society within the show as well. According to one website, you can find articles in the following subjects (and others as well!) that utilize **Buffy** to make their arguments:

- classics
- American studies
- computer science
- folklore
- gender studies
- library science
- intercultural communication
- religious studies/theology
- linguistics
- musicology
- physics

Buffy in her endeavors. He started out his vampiric life as Angelus, but gypsies later cursed him with a soul in order to make him suffer for the many horrible crimes he committed in the hundreds of years he existed.

Angel helps Buffy by showing up at strange times and places, offering her cryptic messages about what's about to happen. Eventually, Angel and Buffy fall in love, although this relationship remains difficult, as none of Buffy's friends can quite trust a vampire. However, their love leads Angel to be happy for the first time since regaining his soul; ironically, this revokes the curse set upon him, and he becomes a normal vampire again. While he is eventually saved by Willow, Buffy's best friend, his relationship with Buffy can never be the same, since they will always fear he will, at some point, become happy again and therefore lose his soul. In the end, Angel leaves because he doesn't want to hurt Buffy any more than he already has, allowing her to get over him and be in a relationship with someone else. Meanwhile, Angel gets his own spin-off show, *Angel*.

Angel might be able to be characterized as one of the "sexy" vampires described in the previous chapter, unlike the majority of vampires in *Buffy*. The attraction viewers feel for him comes from the fact that he has a soul and is tormented between his desire to be with Buffy and his demonic nature. He remains mysterious and tortured, showing us that part of vampire's appeal

is this internal conflict, a conflict that many of us perhaps may feel as well.

## Spike

Spike is another vampire in *Buffy* who is allowed character development and does not come across as purely evil. While he, unlike Angel, continues to enjoy killing people, he has some emotions that other vampires seem not to have. For example, he often has a girl friend around, first Drusilla and later Harmony. He turns his mother into a vampire because she was going to die (compassion is another human emotion that vampires rarely show in *Buffy*), but he later kills her with a stake because he cannot bear to see how soulless and evil she becomes after her conversion.

In the later seasons of the show, Spike is implanted with a chip that keeps him from harming humans without feeling crippling pain himself. This allows him to become more of a fixture on the show, and he falls in love with Buffy. While they eventually have a relationship, it is violent and unhealthy, and it later leads a guilt-stricken Spike to go to Africa in search of his soul. He gets his soul back, and at the end of the show, he sacrifices himself in order to save the world.

Like Angel, Spike is an appealing character because he is allowed to have just enough human characteristics to make his internal struggles seem real. He is not so interesting in the beginning of the series, where he is a one-sided villain who repeatedly tries to kill Buffy and her friends; instead, he becomes more attractive when he is given enough human characteristics to show the audience his struggles with his feelings.

## chapter 4
# TWILIGHT AND BEYOND

Of course, one of the most popular vampire books today is the Twilight series, by Stephanie Meyer. This series, which includes the titles *Twilight*, *New Moon*, *Eclipse*, and *Breaking Dawn*, was released between 2005 and 2008. The vampires in the world of Twilight differ drastically from other vampires in stories; this is partially intentional, but also because Meyer has said that she did not research vampire mythology at all before starting to write the series. Instead, many of the characteristics of vampires in the Twilight world are unique to Meyer. Wooden stakes, crosses, and daylight do not harm them. Instead, the only reason they don't go out in the day is because they sparkle, making their identity obvious to others. Nor do they sleep during the day, as other vampires in stories like *True Blood*, The Vampire Chronicles, and *Dracula* do. Instead, Edward, the main character, is able to watch Bella while she sleeps all night and attend school during the day because he does not require sleep of his own.

In the Twilight series, vampires are extremely beautiful, possessing great physical strength and speed. Their eye color is also unique; most vampires have red eyes, while those who live off animals instead of humans, like the Cullen family, have golden eyes. Many also have supernatural capabilities: Edward can read people's thoughts (except for Bella's), Alice can tell the future, and Jasper can make people feel various emotions. The Twilight vampires are extremely difficult to kill; no stake in the heart will do it. Instead, they must be dismembered and then their limbs burned (to keep their body parts from joining back together).

There are also werewolves in Twilight; Jacob is one of the boys in the Quileute tribe who gained the ability to transform themselves into wolves when vampires are near. These werewolves also differ drastically from the traditional portrayals of were-creatures: Jacob's transformation occurs at will and has nothing to do with the full moon. Nor is his unique ability triggered by another werewolf's bite; instead, it was a change that set upon him like an illness, making him sick but, at the end, able to transform. The pack mentality is also specific to Meyer's book; other stories do not talk about werewolves existing in packs (the exception might be Fenrir Greyback's army in *Harry Potter*). In Twilight's world, the pack of boys all went through the change at roughly the

When you can live forever,
what do you live for?
twilight
IN THEATRES
12·12·08

same time. They hunt and protect their land together and are bound by a telepathic link to the alpha male, Sam Uley.

# Teenage Vampires and Werewolves

Meyer takes many of the themes that are present in the other supernatural literature and adapts them for a teenage audience. Like *Buffy*, she uses vampires to point to the struggles of being a teenager in modern-day America. However, in many ways, Meyer takes an opposite approach. In *Buffy*, creator Joss Whedon attempts to show the female agency of Buffy, who finds her own way in a male-dominated world while trying to overthrow the sexist society in her way. Meyer's approach, it could be argued, is almost exactly the opposite. Bella, the heroine of the Twilight series, is much closer to one of the passive Gothic heroines; one author describes her as the passive recipient of the constant male gaze. Men are constantly looking at her and admiring her, and she is shown as having little ability to act on her own. Instead, she must wait for men, whether it be Edward or Jacob, to save her, both physically and in terms of her mental health as well.

Despite what could be argued is the passivity of the main heroine, the Twilight series is now tremendously

# THE **CULLEN** FAMILY

popular; the books' audience, as well as that of the film versions, reach across many different age groups. Both the books and the films, however, are meant to appeal primarily to teenagers. Earlier in this book, the appeal of vampires was discussed, highlighting the fact that vampires give us space to explore our own issues and problems while placing them outside of ourselves and in the realm of the supernatural. This, it could be argued, is what Meyer has done in a teen setting. The problems of all teenagers—whether it be fitting in at a new school, making friends, breaking up with a significant other, or worries about sex—are all reflected in Meyer's story, although the main characters are vampires and werewolves rather than humans. For example, Edward and Bella's discussions about sex could be applied to any high school couple. Edward worries he might lose control while they are engaged in intimate activity and hurt Bella; he argues that they should wait, while Bella fights for a more physical relationship with Edward.

# Mormonism and Twilight

Stephanie Meyer is a Mormon who graduated from Brigham Young University, and her Mormon worldview can be seen throughout the Twilight novels. For example, in the Mormon faith, family and marriage are extremely important; marriages are believed to be forever and to exist "for time and eternity." Once married, you are married forever, even after death. In a similar way, the vampires in the Twilight series have formed family bonds and marriages, relationships that will last forever, since vampires are immortal. The Cullen family is portrayed as the epitome of a healthy family; while they may not be related by blood, they have found each other and will support each other. Within this family are married

*In creatures of the night, we encounter the hidden darkness of our own natures. We are both terrified and fascinated.*

couples, who are bonded for eternity because of their immortality.

The Cullens, and by extension the relationship between Edward and Bella, are in line with the Mormon ideal family in other ways as well. One example is their free will. They are able to be "vegetarian," or to only eat animals instead of humans. In the Mormon belief structure, this can be related to the idea that all humans have the free will to resist evil and to choose not to sin. When viewed this way, Bella's decision to marry Edward and join the Cullens becomes almost a conversion story, a shift from an unstable family (her parents are divorced) to a marriage in a stable family with good moral values.

While Meyer's vampires and werewolves might differ from the traditional portrayals of supernatural beings in the media, her books illustrate why these creatures are so appealing to our world today. As we use our imaginations to interact with the supernatural, we can examine ourselves and our flaws while pretending these cracks in our characters are totally external—and therefore not as scary or as threatening. We are attracted to these dark creatures of the night because in them we see both the best and the worst aspects of ourselves. Through them, we can fantasize about things we are prevented from doing because of the limits of polite society. We can choose to either slay them—or fall in love with them.

# WORDS YOU MAY NOT KNOW

**agency**: Having the power to act independently.

**agricultural**: Referring to the system of producing food by growing crops and raising animals.

**chaste**: Pure and innocent in thought and action.

**conservative**: Tending to resist change and new ideas.

**domesticated**: Having its wild and unruly nature controlled and tamed.

**dualities**: Pairs of opposite, but related, qualities.

**elite**: The top social and economic class.

**epitome**: The best example of something.

**genre**: A style category in literature, music, or art.

**iconic**: Something that is a well-known symbol of an important cultural idea.

**immortalized**: Having everlasting fame.

**impending**: An event that is about to happen.

**inherent**: A quality or trait that is very basic to something.

**maenad**: A wild-acting female follower of the Greek god Dionysius.

**malevolent**: Producing harm or evil.

**mass-produced**: Created cheaply and in large amounts, usually by a mechanical process.

**passive**: Easily influenced and controlled by other people.

**restitution**: Making up for, or compensating for, loss or damage.

**taboo**: Behaviors that are forbidden by society.

**Victorian**: Referring to the years 1837–1901, the reign of Queen Victoria of Great Britain.

**voluptuous**: Fully enjoying the pleasures of the senses.

# Find Out More on the Internet

Anne Rice's website
http://www.annerice.com

The Homepage for Eclipse (the film)
http://eclipse.test.summit-ent.com/worldoftwilight/#/Home/HTBL/HBR

The Munsters
http://www.munsters.com

Slayage: The International Journal of Buffy Studies
http://www.slayageonline.com

Stephanie Meyer's website
http://www.stepheniemeyer.com/index.html

True Blood website
http://www.hbo.com/true-blood/index.html

# Further Reading

Melton, J. Gordon. *The Vampire Book: The Encyclopedia of the Undead*. Canton, Mich.: Visible Ink Press, 1999.

Meyer, Stephanie. *The Twilight Saga: The Official Guide*. New York: Little, Brown Young Readers, 2010.

Rice, Anne. *Interview with a Vampire*. New York: Random House, Inc., 1976.

Stoker, Bram. *Dracula*. New York: Penguin Books, 2003.

Wilcox, Rhonda V. *Why Buffy Matters: The Art of Buffy the Vampire Slayer*. New York: I.B. Tauris & Co Ltd., 2005.

Wilson, Leah, ed. *A Taste of True Blood: The Fangbanger's Guide*. Dallas, Texas: Smart Pop Books, 2010.

# Bibliography

Abbott, Stacey. "A Little Less Ritual and a Little More Fun: The Modern Vampire in *Buffy the Vampire Slayer*." *Slayer: The Online International Journal of Buffy Studies* 1.3 (June 2001), slayageonline.com/essays/slayage3/sabbott.htm (8 June, 2010).

Clark, Elizabeth M. "'Hairy Thuggish Women': Female Were-wolves, Gender, and the Hoped-for Monster." Masters diss., Georgetown University, 2008.

De Vore, David, Anne Domenic, Alexandra Kwan, and Nicole Reidy. "The Gothic Novel." UC David. cai.ucdavis.edu/waters-sites/gothicnovel/155breport.html (8 June, 2010).

Dime Novel and Story Paper Collection at Stanford. "Dime Novels and Penny Dreadfuls." Stanford University. www.sul. stanford.edu/depts/dp/pennies/home.html (8 June, 2010).

Hammond, Lyn. "Christopher Lee Mini Biography." IMDb. com. www.imdb.com/name/nm0000489/bio (8 June, 2010).

Harry Potter Wiki. harrypotter.wikia.com/wiki/Main_Page (8 June, 2010).

Izzard, Jon. *Werewolves*. London: Spruce, 2009.

Montague, Charlotte. *Vampires from Dracula to Twilight: the Complete Guide to Vampire Mythology*. New York: Chartwell, 2010.

Peterson, Latoya. "The Tyranny of Sexy: Female Werewolves in Pop Culture." *Jezebel: Celebrity, Sex, Fashion for Women* (4 February, 2010), jezebel.com/5461712/the-tyranny-of-sexy-female-werewolves-in-pop-culture (8 June, 2010).

Salamon, Julie. "The Cult of Buffy." *New York Times Upfront* (5 March, 2001), findarticles.com/p/articles/mi_m0BUE/ is_13_133/ai_n18611466/ (8 June, 2010).

Stevens, Kirsten. "Meet the Cullens: Family, Romance and Female Agency in *Buffy the Vampire Slayer and Twilight*." *Slayer: The Online International Journal of Buffy Studies* 8.1 (Spring 2010), slayageonline.com/essays/slayage29/Stevens.htm (8 June, 2010).

Stevenson, Jay. *The Complete Idiot's Guide to Vampires*. Indianapolis, Ind.: Alpha, 2009.

Weeks, Linton. "You Sexy Beast: Our Fascination with Werewolves." NPR. www.npr.org/templates/story/story. php?storyId=106728088 (8 June, 2010).

# Index

# ABOUT THE AUTHOR

Emily Sanna has a degree in religion from Oberlin College. She went on to attend Yale for her master's degree in divinity. She applies her interest in religion to a wide variety of topics, including GLBT issues and the environment—and even vampires! She has written many books for young adults on topics that range from the lives of hip hop stars to the dangers of illicit drugs.

## Picture Credits